KEEPER OF THE CRYSTALS

Eve and the Mermaid's Tears

For Maggie, our mermaid.

First published in the UK in 2017
by New Frontier Publishing Pty Ltd
93 Harbord Street, London SW6 6PN
www.newfrontierpublishing.co.uk

ISBN: 978-1-912076-67-3 (PB)

Illustrations by Celeste Hulme

A CIP catalogue record for this book is available from
the British Library.

Cover illustration and design by Celeste Hulme

Printed in China
10 9 8 7 6 5 4 3 2 1

KEEPER OF THE CRYSTALS

Eve and the Mermaid's Tears

Jess Black

Illustrated by Celeste Hulme

'ARRRRRRRR!'

Eve was startled by a loud shout from behind. She swung around to see her friend Oscar in full fight mode. He was barely recognisable in black pants, a leather waistcoat, a bandana around his head and a black patch over one eye. Oscar pointed a plastic sword at Eve before adding a few playful thrusts in her direction.

Eve burst out laughing.

'Cursed wench!' Oscar growled.

Eve and Oscar were inside the maritime museum in the small seaside town of Marigold. The museum only opened one day a month and Oscar had been keen to show Eve around. All things pirates were big with Oscar.

'Hand over your jewels, landlubber!' he yelled.

'I have bad news for you, Oscar,' Eve giggled. 'You're not very scary.'

'Watch how you talk to Captain Blood, me girl,' Oscar cocked his head and snarled.

'Captain Blood?' Eve snorted. 'Captain Faint-at-the-Sight-of-Blood, more like.'

'We'll see how funny it is when you're walkin' the plank!' Oscar cut, thrust and parried an imaginary blow then prodded Eve with the end of his plastic sword.

Eve shrieked.

A tug of war for the sword led to the two friends collapsing on the floor in a wrestling match. Two elderly women entered the room and glared at them with disapproval.

'Shhh!' one of the women said, holding a finger to her lips. 'No noise in the museum!'

In a fit of giggles Eve and Oscar took off down one of the long corridors that led to another display hall.

'Yo ho ho and a bottle of rum!' Oscar sang in what he thought sounded like a swashbuckling tune.

'*Shhh*!' Eve mimicked the cross woman. 'You'll get us thrown out.'

'That'll make a change!' Oscar teased her. 'It's usually *you* getting us into trouble.'

Eve smiled at the memory of the many sticky situations she and Oscar had found themselves in. Oscar lived next door to

Eve's grandmother Sylvie. Eve had never really liked coming to Marigold for holidays until the day she and Oscar had accidentally discovered a portal into another world. Since then they had had many adventures together in different lands and faced many dangers. They were now great friends and Eve looked forward to every holiday at her gran's.

The giggling pair raced each other around the museum, passing glass cabinets filled with models of shipwrecks and old nautical maps. Eve tore around a corner and nearly collided with an enormous pair of legs. She screeched to an abrupt halt which caused Oscar to collide with her from behind.

'Oof! Ouch!' Oscar rubbed his head, then noticed the bulky man blocking Eve's way. The legs belonged to a grizzled old man with a full beard. The beard had once been

red but was now flecked with grey which gave it a rusty appearance. He was tall and solidly built.

'Slow down there, lassie.' The man growled more than spoke. 'Hmmm. Sylvie's granddaughter?'

'Eve, sir ... ' Eve managed to say. All thoughts of games and laughter vanished.

The man was dressed in all-weather gear like a sailor or a fisherman and Eve noted his enormous booted legs were not a matching pair. Where his left foot should have been was a wooden stump.

'It's all fun and games until some fool boy loses an eye.' He locked eyes with Oscar, who gulped. 'A pirate's life isn't all it's cracked up to be, you know. You should ask this lassie's grandmother about that!' The man's face broke into a smile. He sauntered away and his booming laugh

echoed down the halls of the museum.

'Let's get out of here,' Eve hissed. Oscar nodded. He hastily took off his pirate costume and stuffed it into the dress-up box on their way out.

***

Outside the sun was shining and Oscar and Eve still had the rest of the day stretching ahead of them.

'What now?' Eve asked.

With thoughts of pirates fresh in his mind, Oscar suggested they check out the old shipwreck up in Black Bay. The town of Marigold was nestled between thick Australian bush and the coastline. There was one beach that was great for swimming but the rest of the coast was not very welcoming for ships or swimmers, with treacherous

rocks and steep headlands.

The old wreckage was the stuff of legends and local kids loved to make up new stories about hauntings, pirates and, most of all, treasure. Black Bay, where the old coaster cargo ship lay, was strictly out of bounds for Eve and Oscar. That didn't stop them.

'There she is – old SS *Penrose*.' Oscar pointed out the tip of the wreckage as it came into view. The rusted remains of the old wheelhouse still stood out at low tide.

'Do you think there was gold on board?' Eve wondered. It all sounded very romantic to her.

Oscar shrugged. 'More like sheep cargo from the stories your gran has told me.'

At the mention of her gran Eve bristled. She and Sylvie hadn't been getting on very well. Eve had pushed Sylvie to tell her more about the crystal power that allowed Eve to

travel to other worlds. Sylvie had clammed up and refused to tell her anything. They had argued the previous night and Eve hadn't spoken to her since.

Eve sighed and made her way out onto the rock shelf that was visible only at low tide.

'Watch out for slippery rocks,' Oscar warned her, following more carefully.

Eve gazed at the sparkling turquoise water beyond the rocks. As she stared, she saw something glistening beneath the surface.

'Hey! What's that?' Eve pointed down to the water.

Oscar leaned forward warily. 'I don't see anything. Come on, let's go. I'm starving.'

Eve followed Oscar but something made her hesitate. As she turned and walked back to the water, she saw a flash of light.

'There *is* something down there,' Eve exclaimed. 'Maybe it's treasure!'

Oscar groaned. 'I never should have taken you to the museum. Too much talk of pirates.'

Eve was wearing her swimsuit, so she flung her sundress onto the rocks and kicked off her sandals. She stepped carefully up onto one of the larger rocks that dropped straight into the ocean.

'You're not … '

'Watch me!' Eve leaped off the boulder and fell into the sea below with a huge splash. The water was cool and refreshing.

'Come on in!' Eve called.

Oscar shook his head and glared at her. Eve took a deep breath and duck-dived under the water. She swam breaststroke down towards the ocean floor. The water was very clear and not deep in this part of the bay. Eve could see seaweed, rocks, a few small fish and tiny clumps of colourful coral.

As she was searching the sun came out from behind a cloud and a streak of light pierced the water. A glint caught her eye and Eve swam towards it. She crouched down under the water, squatting on some rocks as her hands searched among the seaweed for the treasure.

But the surface was slippery and Eve's foot slipped into a small crevice between two rocks. When she tried to pull her leg out she realised her ankle was caught.

Eve strained and pulled at her leg. She twisted around but it was no use.

Her foot was caught and she was stuck at the bottom of the sea.

Eve tried desperately to free herself by feeling her way around the rock. She tried to stay calm and not use up her air. She and Oscar often challenged each other to breath-holding competitions. She felt sure Oscar would come to help.

As Eve kicked away a clump of seaweed with her free leg, it revealed the shining object she had seen from above the water.

It was a crystal.

Eve knew immediately that it was a magic crystal, just like the others that had transported her and Oscar to other worlds. This one was shaped like a mermaid. Eve strained to touch it but it was just out of reach.

Eve began to feel light-headed and faint. She couldn't hold her breath for much longer.

Then Oscar appeared, swimming towards her powerfully with a look of fear on his face. She pointed madly to the crystal lying half-hidden in the sand.

Oscar reached down and picked up the small object. He put the mermaid in Eve's hand and folded her fingers around it.

A familiar surge raced through Eve's body. Her body tingled and the hand that held the crystal burned with an intense

heat. The magic was working! The water around Eve and Oscar lit up brightly and a dazzling stream of coloured light shone out in all directions. Everything looked sharper and the colours were more intense.

With a start Eve realised she could breathe. Was she breathing underwater? She squeezed Oscar's hand and smiled at him. Her foot seemed to glide free of the rock. Oscar still looked worried and pointed to the surface. He needed to get some air.

'Go!' Eve mouthed, and Oscar shot to the surface.

As she followed Oscar, Eve saw a large green fin flick past her. She froze. The enormous green and blue tail snaked its way closer. Suddenly Eve was staring at a young woman. But the woman was only half-human. The tail was hers. Her pale face was surrounded by a tangle of beautiful

long brown hair, and her body was covered in what looked like tiny silver plates. As she swam closer, Eve saw they were fishy scales that stretched from just above her chest all the way down to her tail. Around her neck she wore a dazzling necklace of green, blue and silver sea glass.

Yikes! A mermaid! Eve thought.

The mermaid was huge. If she'd had legs she would have been taller than any man Eve had met. Her arms were strong and muscular and Eve noticed that she had green fingernails.

Eve gazed up at the creature in admiration and fear. The woman looked imploringly at Eve.

Help us.

Eve heard the words even though the mermaid had not spoken out loud.

She looked into the mermaid's eyes. It was

like gazing into an enormous dark green pool. The more Eve looked, the more she felt she was falling into some kind of trance. Thousands of tiny luminescent bubbles cascaded around the mermaid. Then she was gone.

Eve suddenly felt wide awake. She swam to the surface to find Oscar. When she reached him she saw straightaway that he was really freaked out.

'What's wrong?'

'Notice anything different?' he asked, a catch in his voice.

Eve followed his gaze and saw only sea. She swung around, looking for the headland and the ship wreck. But they were no longer there. Neither was the town of Marigold. There was only endless water stretching to the horizon in all directions. The water was different too. It was warm and tropical, and

a paler blue. They were now in a completely different place.

'The mermaid's magic?' Eve tried to make sense of it as she kept herself afloat. 'We're in another world.'

'Sea World?' Oscar joked but then looked serious. 'We've been in all kinds of trouble in different worlds but being stuck in the middle of the ocean is no joke. There could be sharks here. All kinds of crazy fish.'

'I saw a mermaid down there, a real one. She asked for help but then swam off.'

'I wonder why she took off if she needs us?' Oscar said. He looked around warily for any sign of a fin or ripple in the water.

'I feel ... strange,' Eve said slowly.

It wasn't just the environment around them that had changed. Eve felt different. Something was changing her too.

Just as Eve had the thought her hand

throbbed. She felt the magic before she saw it.

'Something is wrong, Oscar!' Eve recognised the familiar jolt of energy but this time it felt all wrong.

'What do you mean?' Oscar asked, swimming over to her. 'Eve? What's happening?'

Where her ribs and swimsuit had been Eve felt sharp scales. With alarm she patted her whole torso and chest and realised she was completely covered in them. She looked down at her body beneath the water and gasped.

Where her legs had been was now a long, silver, shimmering mermaid's tail.

'Eve? Eve! What is it?'

'Promise me you won't freak out?' she asked Oscar in a small voice.

Oscar's eyes widened. 'You mean freak out any more than I already have?'

Eve nodded. 'Stick your head underwater and tell me if you notice anything different.'

'Eve, this is no time for mucking around,' Oscar frowned.

'Just do it. Please?'

Oscar took a breath and disappeared under the water. Almost immediately he shot back up.

'Are you kidding me? You don't have any legs!' Now Oscar looked *really* freaked out.

'And I can breathe underwater,' Eve said. She held her hand up to him. On her palm was the bold black outline of a mermaid.

Oscar shook his head in bewilderment. 'So I'm treading water in the middle of the ocean with a mermaid as a best friend,' he mused. 'Oh well. Things could be worse.'

Eve giggled. Now that the shock was wearing off she felt a thrill of excitement. 'It's like a dream come true. I'm a real mermaid!' She looked down at her glittering body and gave her tail a small flick. She flew through the water with such sudden speed that she somersaulted and came up with a splash.

'Wow. I'm really fast!'

'Awesome! Do it again,' called Oscar with enthusiasm.

Eve tested her speed and found she could shoot across the water swiftly in any direction. She tried a few somersaults and once she got the hang of breathing underwater she began to feel at home in her new body. It felt as if she was wearing supersonic flippers. One kick from her powerful tail sent her darting through the water, creating little ripples in her wake.

'You'd get a job at the aquarium, no problem,' Oscar teased, then turned serious as the endless water view reminded him of their situation. 'We are still stuck in the middle of the ocean, though. We need to find out why we're here. Can you try calling the mermaid?'

'Good idea,' Eve replied. After their adventures in Panthor and Griffid, Eve

knew she had a link to any creature who had called them to help. Having the mark of a mermaid on her hand and now being a mermaid herself meant that the mermaids were in some kind of trouble.

Eve rubbed her palm and traced the outline with her finger. She pictured the woman's face in her mind.

Thank you for saving me but now we're a little lost. Where are we? Can you help us?

She felt a slight vibration from the mermaid but it was very weak.

'I think the mermaid's in trouble,' Eve said, worried.

'I see something.' Oscar pointed towards a tiny object in the distance. 'What's that?'

Eve squinted in the direction Oscar was pointing. Far away on the horizon was something that looked like a sail.

'A ship!' Oscar cried with excitement.

The sail grew more and more defined, and soon they could see the whole vessel.

'It looks just like the ship we saw in the museum,' Eve noted.

'It's a single-masted sloop,' Oscar said in awe. 'See the shallow hull? It makes them easy to manoeuvre.

'If you say so,' muttered Eve. 'Looks like an old ship to me.'

'It's a beauty. Look how fast it is. Needs only a small crew.'

The ship drew closer. It was as if a model from the maritime museum had come to life. The sails were old-fashioned and made of thick cream-coloured cloth.

'What were sloops used for?' Eve asked.

'All kinds of things. The navy used them. Although if this was a naval rig there would be two or more sails and it would be a bigger ship ... '

A shift in the breeze caused the ship to change tack. Instead of seeing it front-on Eve and Oscar now gazed at the ship from the side.

'Oscar, who else used sloops?' Eve asked.

Oscar went pale. 'Smugglers, and ... '

They looked up to the top of the mast and saw the black flag unfurled in the breeze. On it was a white skull and crossbones.

' ... pirates!'

Eve and Oscar stared in horror as the ship drew closer. What had first looked quaint and welcoming now looked eerie and dangerous.

They were sitting ducks in the water, just waiting and watching.

Can you help us please? Eve spoke to the mermaid again. This time there was no answer at all.

The ship drew closer. Oscar was right. It was fast. Eve watched a man climb the rigging. He saw them immediately and gave a shout. The ship gained speed and bore down on them.

'I was only joking when I said I wanted to be a pirate,' said Oscar shakily.

There was nowhere to hide. A swarm of seagulls screeched and circled above their heads and around the ship. Eve could hear the sails flapping and rustling and the slow creak of the mast. The sound sent shivers down Eve's spine. She counted at least ten men, all dressed in black.

They could see a net strung up from the mast over the deck. There was something writhing inside. The rope creaked as it was tightened and the men cheered. The struggling creature inside the net wasn't a dolphin or a shark.

Eve gulped. It was the mermaid.

'We have to help her,' Eve cried.

'Get underwater, Eve. You can get away!' Oscar said quickly.

'Don't be silly, I'm not leaving you,' Eve snapped, just as a thick and heavy net was flung down on their heads. The netting swept them up. All too soon they were being dragged out of the water and hauled up the side of the ship.

As Eve and Oscar left the water, Eve looked down to see her tail vanishing before her eyes. She had legs again! Her body was adapting to being in and out of the water.

Two men hauled on the ropes. They were deeply tanned with grubby faces, chapped skin and peeling lips. Both had long scruffy beards and one of them had a nasty scar across most of his forehead. 'Come to Daddy!' shouted Scarface as the net was

jerked ever closer.

'Have you got your Swiss Army knife?' Eve whispered.

Oscar's eyes lit up. He patted his soggy shorts pocket and felt for the trusty tool. He nodded.

'Hurry!' hissed Eve.

Oscar began sawing at the thick hemp with all his might but it was tough going and his blade hardly made a mark. He tried again.

'Keep away from us!' Eve called to the men in a voice that sounded much braver than she felt.

'Oh, I'm trembling!' Scarface snorted and then laughed. Eve could see his rotted teeth as they inched their way closer to the deck.

Another pirate who was unmistakably the captain was watching them from the upper deck. This man had an ugly red welt

across his cheek and long black hair that fell untidily around his shoulders. But what really marked him as different from the others was the intensity of his gaze. His dark eyes bore into Eve.

'Hurry Oscar!' Eve gulped.

'Nearly there,' Oscar whispered as beads of sweat gathered on his brow. Where his knife was cutting strands of twine were unravelling and only a few remained.

The net finally drew level with the ship's rail. Scarface leaned over and grabbed hold of it. Eve and Oscar scrambled as far away from his huge hand as possible, but the pirate managed to grab hold of Eve's hair.

Before she thought twice about what she was doing she twisted around and bit down hard on his knuckle.

'Argh! You little no-good ... ' Scarface swore and reached his other hand into

the net. At the same moment the rope finally gave way under Oscar's sawing and Eve wriggled through the small hole and dropped into the water.

'Go Eve! Go!' Oscar yelled as he was grabbed by two burly pirates. 'Get away!'

'Oscar!' Eve called. She felt the surge of energy again and was transformed back into mermaid form.

Eve didn't want to leave Oscar but she knew he was right. It would do no good for them both to be captured.

'I'll come back for you. I'll find a way!'

Eve gave her tail a strong flick and swam away from the ship as fast as she could.

The next few hours were very lonely for Eve. She kept the ship in sight but made sure not to get too close. In all of their adventures together Eve and Oscar had never been separated. Eve realised how much she relied on Oscar. Now it was all up to Eve but she had no idea what to do.

Eve hardly ever cried but she felt like

crying now. The only thing that stopped the tears from falling was that she hated the idea of those pirates making her cry.

Finally, as the sun dipped lower in the sky, the pirates dropped anchor and moored the ship for the night.

'Hang in there Oscar,' Eve said quietly as she watched the ship's shadowy hulk. 'I'll get you out of there. I just have to figure out how.'

'Maybe we can help each other,' said a voice in the darkness near her.

'Ah!' Eve splashed in fright and shot a few metres away. Turning around, she saw another mermaid in the water. In the dim light she looked very much like the mermaid who had rescued Eve, but she was older and her skin had a green tinge to it.

'Oh!' Eve breathed out. 'You scared me.'

'Sorry. I didn't know how else to introduce

myself.' The corners of her mouth turned up in a smile. 'I know I shouldn't laugh but you should have seen your face.'

Despite herself Eve smiled too. 'It's been a difficult day.'

'Yes, I know. My name is Lyla,' the mermaid said gently.

'I'm Eve,' said Eve. 'Before today I was an ordinary human but right now I have a tail.'

Lyla nodded approvingly. 'A fine one it is too.'

'My friend Oscar was captured by ... '

' ... pirates. I know.' Lyla cut Eve off, looking vexed at the mention of the word. 'They have taken one of us too – Pearl, the mermaid you saw earlier. They have been doing this for a while now. We need your help, Eve. If there are not enough of us in the ocean we can't do our job properly. We are protectors of all who live in our world –

the world of the Serenade Sea.'

'Protectors? How?'

'We help keep all marine life safe from humans. If too much fishing threatens to wipe out a whole species, or if there is pollution from ships and rubbish dumped in the ocean, we can fix it or clean it up. We have mermaid protectors everywhere in the ocean and by working together we keep the underwater world in balance.'

'But why are the pirates kidnapping you?'

Lyla fingered a strand of beads around her neck. 'It's because of this.'

The necklace was a beautiful strand of sea glass made up of beads in shades of turquoise and green. Each bead was perfectly formed and sparkled even in the dimming light. It was luminous.

'Is it worth a lot of money?'

'It is priceless. Each necklace is unique

to the mermaid who wears it. It is created from the tears of a mermaid when she first cries. The magic of the necklace is very powerful and very old. It can be used for almost anything. You can change the weather, make gold. The pirates are using magic to make sailing easier, to create fast winds and storms, even to make their own money. They grow more and more greedy and powerful.'

'*That's* why the pirates want the mermaids? To use the magic?'

Lyla nodded. 'Once they have the jewels the mermaids are discarded. If we are kept out of the water for too long we cannot survive.'

'That's terrible!' Eve gasped. 'What can we do?'

'I know where the pirates are heading,' Lyla continued. 'It's called Pirate Inlet, on

one of the Tripod Islands. If we hurry we can get there before them. If we can take them by surprise we might be able to rescue Pearl and Oscar. Perhaps together our magic will be strong enough to overthrow the pirates completely. In the old magic, the mermaids call on one who is part mermaid, part human – a being with very powerful magic. That is *you*, Eve.'

It took a moment for Eve to digest the information.

'What do they want with Oscar?' Eve asked.

'They want you. Maybe they know you will come for your friend.' Lyla shrugged. 'They might force him to work as a deckhand on the ship. Or they might get him to walk the plank.'

The two mermaids fell silent at the thought.

'What do you think?' Lyla asked. 'Are you up for this?'

'Sounds like a plan,' Eve said firmly. She was relieved to have Lyla's company and a plan of action.

'There's a slight problem.' A frown creased Lyla's forehead. 'In order to reach the islands we have to cross the Sarosa Sea.'

'What's the catch?'

'The Sarosa Seaweed. It's lethal. If you get caught up in it you'll never get away. The seaweed acts as a kind of spider's web. It holds its prey and slowly feeds on it until nothing is left.'

Eve shuddered. 'Can't you use your magic?' she asked.

'Mermaids cannot change the balance of the natural world. We can't upset the ocean's ecosystem. The weed has as much right to live here as a mermaid, a shark or a

whale – or any other creature.'

Eve realised that being a mermaid was not all about sitting on rocks and singing to sailors. Danger lurked at every turn.

'If there's no other way to get to Oscar we have to try it,' Eve decided.

***

Eve and Lyla swam quietly in the twilight until Lyla suddenly held out a webbed hand and motioned for Eve to stop. 'We are near,' she said softly.

Up ahead Eve could see the thick Sarosa Seaweed. Even in the dark she could see that it covered the water like a black blanket and waved from side to side with the current.

'Stay close. Use long and lazy tail kicks in the channel but when we reach the weed you need to drift with the current. Okay?'

A sudden scuffle in the water drew their attention. A small stingray had been chasing prey and drifted too close to the weed. The weed enveloped the ray and despite the creature's struggling it was pulled onto the weed's web. The ray disappeared completely.

Lyla met Eve's eyes, then pointed ahead. 'We swim for that gap. The only way to get through is to make absolutely no movement so that you float on the current and pass through the gaps. The tide is moving that way and I think we have a chance.'

Eve could see a thin break in the weed. It looked tiny, but it was the only way.

'I'm ready,' Eve nodded. Oscar needed her.

6

Eve could feel her body tense up as she moved closer to the seaweed's oily tendrils. As her body drifted into the gap the slimy weed brushed against her skin. It took all of her nerve not to cry out. Small sticky fronds covered in suction cups explored her skin and hair.

Eve's mouth felt dry. Her thoughts went to her gran. They had argued and they never

argued. Eve felt a pang of guilt at the way she had spoken to Sylvie.

The weed was thick and suffocating. Eve couldn't take it anymore. She flicked her fin to get away from the slimy suckers.

The weed reacted to her movement immediately. Eve's body was covered in tendrils that snaked around her arms, tail and torso. Then they squeezed. Eve was bound tight and unable to move.

'Lyla!' Eve managed to call out just as her voice was muffled by a slippery leech-like tendril covering her lips. She nearly gagged.

'Don't struggle,' Lyla called to her. She had made it safely to the other side of the weed and hovered at a distance. 'You have to trust me, Eve. Don't move a muscle.'

Ever since she was a little girl Eve had hated confined spaces. Her cousin Rory had locked her in her parents' cupboard once

when she was six and nobody had found her for hours. She had cried herself to sleep curled up among her father's shoes.

'You won't get me,' Eve thought as the tendrils gripped her body. Oscar needed her. She slowed down her breathing and turned her thoughts to something else. Eve remembered her mother teaching her to swim and how she'd held Eve tightly in the pool.

'It's okay, Mum,' Eve had said. 'You can let me go now.'

Her mum had forced a smile and gradually allowed the water to support Eve's weight. Eve had been so relaxed that she had floated on her own. Her mum's smile became a genuine one. It was one of Eve's favourite memories.

Eve opened her eyes to find that the last tendrils had relaxed their grip and she had

passed through to the other side of the weed.

Lyla hugged her. 'You did it!'

Eve smiled weakly. It was a relief to know she wouldn't be a giant weed's dinner for the next few years.

***

They swam on through the night. Eve had expected the sea to be dark and gloomy but soon the darkness transformed the water into a brightly coloured wonderland. The seaweed and coral they passed were more beautiful than any fireworks display Eve had ever seen. Schools of multi-coloured and neon fish swam around them.

They met plenty of other marine life as they travelled on through the next day. Eve marvelled at Lyla's gentle approach and the

way she was able to speak with any creature they passed.

As night approached again they finally arrived at Pirate Inlet. They had travelled nonstop for a whole night and day.

Lyla found a secluded bay and pointed upwards. They swam to the surface. It felt odd to Eve to stick her head above water and breathe air again. She could feel her gills adjusting and her lungs taking over.

'The ship is still a few hours away. We made good time.' Lyla looked relieved but tired. There were deep creases at the sides of her eyes and her skin had turned a deeper shade of green. 'Let's try to sleep. We will need our strength.'

'I can hardly keep my eyes open,' Eve admitted.

Eve realised she was exhausted. Her back and shoulder muscles ached from the

unusual swimming style. She felt completely waterlogged. 'How do mermaids sleep?'

Lyla laughed. 'Like all marine life, of course!' Lyla noticed Eve's look of confusion. 'We close our eyes and hey presto!'

Within minutes they were both asleep.

***

Eve woke with a start. The mark of the mermaid on her palm was throbbing and her hand ached. Lyla was nowhere to be seen.

Eve had no idea how long she had slept underwater. She swam to the surface. There was only a sliver of moon and the few small fishermen's cottages in the cove were in darkness.

Where are you, Lyla? Eve thought. She tried to communicate with Lyla but received no answer.

A familiar sound sent a chill down Eve's spine. There was no mistaking the loud flap of the large billowing sails of the pirate ship. It was moored in the shallow bay of Pirate Inlet. Its looming shape created a chilling shadow.

'Pirates,' Eve whispered. 'We meet again.'

7

Eve swam cautiously into the harbour and approached the ship from underwater. She felt her way along the mossy, encrusted hull until she reached the decorative carving under the bow and surfaced. All appeared quiet on board. Eve hoped the pirates were all deeply asleep.

Now to find a way on board, she thought.

Eve saw a net hanging over the side of

the ship. It wasn't as large as the net she had been caught in, but if it was attached to something she could use it as a ladder. She gave it a firm tug and it held. As she climbed up stealthily her tail vanished and her bare legs shone in the pale light.

Eve straddled the railing and slipped silently onto the deck. A shabby pirate who looked as if he was meant to be keeping watch had fallen asleep in a hammock strung from the mast.

Eve adjusted her balance to the sway of the deck underfoot. The light from an overhanging lantern created confusing shadows as it swung in the breeze. The whole ship smelled of an unpleasant mixture of sweat, salted fish and pungent kerosene from the burning lamp.

Eve crept down a narrow flight of stairs and into the lower bilge. She hesitated when

she saw two pirates slumped in the narrow corridor but their hearty snores reassured her. She noticed one of them was Scarface. Even fast asleep he looked mean, his salt-worn face fixed in a scowl. Eve carefully stepped over them.

Eve continued on and entered the ship's galley. She sucked in her breath as she saw a familiar face between thick metal bars.

'Oscar!' she whispered.

Oscar was asleep, curled up on the dirty floor of a cell in the corner of the galley. His face was sunburned and streaked with dirt but he looked okay. Lying alongside him was a young girl. Eve recognised her as Pearl, the mermaid who had found her when she'd first touched the crystal.

'Oscar!' Eve whispered again. 'Wake up!' She stuck her arm though the bars and gave his shoulder a squeeze.

Oscar woke with a start. 'Stay away from her!' he croaked, still half-asleep.

'Shhh!' Eve put her hand over his mouth. 'It's me. Eve.'

Oscar sat up abruptly, eyes wide. 'Eve ... ' Oscar's whisper trailed off. 'How did you get here?'

'I came with another mermaid, Lyla. Have you seen her?'

Oscar shook his head, clearly confused. 'It's just me and Pearl on board. They're going to sell her tomorrow. Something about her tears being worth more than gold.'

Eve nodded. 'The first time a mermaid cries their tears form a necklace. It's their magic talisman. It allows them to do their job of protecting the ocean.' Eve pointed to the necklace around Pearl's neck. 'That's what they want. So we need to get you both out of here.' She tried the handle of the cell

but the door was firmly locked.

Oscar pointed to a sleeping figure in the opposite corner of the galley. 'That's Roche. He's got the key on his belt. He's the ship's cook but he's not a very good pirate. He's been sneaking seawater to pour over Pearl. If they don't keep wet they get really sick. We need to get her back into the sea.'

Eve tiptoed over to the cook. A small brass key hung from a hook attached to his belt buckle. Eve took a deep breath and reached for the key. It was firmly attached.

The cook's eyes flew open. He grabbed Eve's arm and held it tight.

'Who do we have here?' he growled.

'I've come for Oscar and Pearl,' Eve replied in a stern whisper.

Roche eyeballed Eve before giving a terse nod. 'It'll be my head, but I don't sit well with torturing sea lasses. You lot get off this

ship and get away fast, you hear?'

His breath smelled of rotten fish and sour wine but Eve gave him a quick hug. 'Thank you.'

He pressed the key into Eve's hand. 'Get out of here quick now, before one of 'em wakes up.' He gave Eve a wink before closing his eyes and letting out a series of loud snores.

Eve rushed to unlock the small steel door. The key turned in the lock with a soft clunk. Oscar scooped up Pearl and carried her in his arms through the small doorway. Then Eve grabbed her legs. There was no time to lose.

Oscar clambered up the ladder from the lower deck, holding Pearl under the arms, and stuck his head out from the top of the ladder. He nodded to Eve and stepped onto the deck, pulling Pearl with him.

The sun was peeking out over the horizon but the pirate on lookout duty still seemed to be fast asleep. Would the sun wake him?

They quietly shuffled across the deck with Pearl slumped between them.

'Let's heave-ho her overboard,' Oscar whispered. Eve moved towards the railing.

'Not so fast, girlie.'

Eve spun around at the gruff voice behind her. The pirate captain was stamping towards them. 'Don't go throwing my riches away or you'll make me very angry.'

'Quick, Oscar!' Eve swung Pearl's feet and they lifted her slumped form over the railing and into the water. Eve saw a splash, then the flick of a tail as Pearl transformed back into mermaid form and sped away.

'You're going to regret that!' The captain slammed his fist down hard on a nearby barrel. The wood cracked and splintered.

'I'm not afraid of you,' Eve challenged.

The captain sneered and the mark across his cheek grew red and angry. 'No? You should be.'

He held up a beautiful mermaid's necklace. The glass sparkled in the early morning light. It was Lyla's.

The captain pointed to the mainsail and there, tied to the mast, was Lyla.

8

Eve sucked in her breath. 'Lyla!'

Lyla looked terrible. Her skin was deathly pale and there were cuts on her hands. But what really shocked Eve was the big gash right across both of Lyla's legs. Her legs hung limply from her slumped body.

The captain read Eve's mind.

'Your mermaid friend will never swim

again,' he gloated. 'Unless she has her magic necklace to heal her.' He dangled the necklace in front of Eve.

Lyla opened her eyes. 'Get away, Eve, while you still can,' she said weakly.

Eve stomped her foot stubbornly. 'No. This is my fault. I brought you here.'

More pirates stumbled on deck and quickly took stock of the situation. They drew their cutlasses and moved towards Oscar and Eve. Oscar backed away. He and Eve were surrounded.

'Don't come a step closer!' Oscar growled with venom. He pulled his Swiss Army knife out of his pocket and waved it. Two of the pirates laughed.

'Enough childish games!' the captain exploded. 'Tie them up!'

From the sail overhead two pirates flew down on ropes. They landed on top of

Oscar, knocking him to the ground. His knife slipped out of his grasp. It skidded across the deck and into the water.

At the same time Scarface grabbed Eve. He bound her arms and feet with rope and tied her to the mast with Lyla. They stood back to back.

'Captain!' Another pirate pushed Roche forward. The cook's hands were tied but he held his head high. The captain spat at him. 'You're a terrible cook and a traitor! You can go overboard with this lot.'

Eve struggled against the ropes but she was held tight. She could only watch helplessly as Oscar was also tied up, his hands and feet firmly bound.

'Send the boy overboard!' roared the captain. Oscar struggled in vain.

Scarface looked at Eve with a cruel smile on his face. 'Say goodbye to your little friend.'

'Oscar!' Eve cried out. She caught Oscar's eye.

The pirates picked Oscar up and threw him over the railing.

He was gone.

'*No!*' Eve shouted and fought to free herself. Not Oscar. Her eyes filled with moisture and a small tear rolled down her cheek.

'Crying like a baby,' crooned the captain. 'Don't worry, it'll be your turn soon.'

Eve felt completely hollow. She tasted the salty bitterness of her tear as it touched her lips. Another tear joined the first and Eve was crying properly for the first time in years.

As the pirates wrapped the ropes around Roche, he looked up at Eve on the mast and suddenly gaped. Then she saw what he saw. Small pieces of bright light like fireflies were

fizzing and popping in the air around her.

Lyla strained her neck to see Eve.

'You're crying … ' Lyla began to laugh with disbelief. 'The magic!'

Eve watched as the dazzling display of magical lights crystallised into perfect glass beads. They were coloured with the blue and green hues of the sea. Eve felt a fusion of energy as the beads collected together in front of her eyes. The mark of the mermaid on Eve's hand glowed and Eve felt a cool pressure around her neck.

'A necklace is forming!' Lyla whispered.

Eve was dimly aware of the captain's shock. The crew stood still, stunned by the lightshow.

'Throw her overboard!' the captain cried but the men remained still.

The sea glass formed into a long strand and wrapped itself around Eve's neck. She

felt a powerful surge and in her mind's eye she saw the eternal history of the mermaids. With great power came great responsibility. She too was a protector of the ocean and everything in it.

'Eve, there is no time to lose. You must get Oscar!' Lyla urged.

Eve didn't need to be reminded. She knew what to do. The ropes that bound her and Lyla fell loosely to the ground. Lyla's trembling legs managed to remain standing. There was an explosion of colour and sound. Eve traced the perfectly formed beads with her fingertips and a bright light radiated from the necklace.

The captain and the other pirates found themselves strung up by their ankles and hanging from a sail. 'Why, you little minx!' the captain yelled as he swung red-faced in the air.

Roche's ropes had also fallen away. He stumbled over to the rail and looked into the water.

Eve held out her palm. As she lifted her arm the water on one side of the ship rose with it. The ship began to rock violently and they were all thrown to one side. A massive wall of water loomed above them.

'There!' Lyla cried, pointing to the water. 'He's with Pearl!'

Sure enough, there were two bodies in the water. Pearl was holding Oscar's slumped form above the surface.

Eve let her arm fall to her side and the water fell away. Pearl and Oscar landed on the deck of the ship. Oscar's eyes were closed and he lay very still.

Eve raced to her friend's side.

Eve put her head on Oscar's chest. Was he breathing?

'Come on Oscar!' Eve willed her friend to be okay.

Oscar coughed and seawater dribbled from his mouth. He coughed again and rolled over onto his side.

'Welcome back,' Eve sighed with relief.

Oscar groaned and offered her a weak

smile. 'Cut me loose, eh, lass?'

Pearl moved forward with Oscar's knife. 'I caught it just in time. And then I caught him,' she laughed gently.

Eve nodded and wasted no time in freeing Oscar's hands and feet.

Despite hanging upside down and swinging in the wind, the captain remained defiant. 'I will not be made into a fool by urchins!' At that moment something fell from his pocket and landed on the deck with a loud clunk. It was Lyla's necklace. Eve's eyes lit up as she picked up the treasure. A furious captain spat out a huge gob of saliva that landed at Eve's feet.

'Eeew,' said Eve in a low voice. 'Someone needs to learn some manners.'

She thought for a moment. 'Roche, can you steer the ship?'

Roche's eyes shone. 'Can I ever!' He

nodded vigorously several times.

'Take the wheel,' Eve commanded.

'I'll need manpower,' Roche pointed out. 'The ship can't sail itself.'

Eve touched her necklace. 'Manpower? I have all the power we'll need right here.'

'Aye aye captain!' Roche scuttled over to the upper deck.

Eve held the necklace out to Lyla. The mermaid took it with trembling fingers and Pearl helped her to tie it around her neck.

Lyla closed her eyes and held onto her necklace. A bolt of white light shot out of the beads and wound itself around Lyla's legs. Her injuries were healed using the mermaid's magic. Lyla whooped in delight. She nodded to Pearl and the two of them leaped over the rail and into the water, whirling and diving with delight.

Eve and Oscar watched happily from the

deck. 'Lyla, I think these scoundrels need a holiday,' Eve called down to her. 'Do you know of any remote islands nearby where they can take a break from pillaging?'

Lyla laughed. 'I know just the place!'

***

They sailed the sloop across the high seas for two days. Using her mermaid magic Eve was able to make the pirates work to sail the ship. Roche taught Oscar how to take charge and by the end of the first day Oscar was able to command the helm.

They finally arrived at a small island far away from any other land. Eve took in the picture postcard view of palm trees, bleached sand and mountains. 'I think the captain and his merry men will love living here.'

'Aren't you worried they'll swim away?'

asked Oscar.

‘Small problem there,’ smiled Lyla. ‘This whole bay is surrounded by Sarosa Seaweed. They’re not going anywhere.’

The motley group of pirates was bundled into the water and left to swim for shore. Pearl followed to make sure that they made it to the island in one piece.

‘Happy holidays!’ Eve waved goodbye to the pirates.

‘Good riddance!’ Oscar called.

‘There’s something I want to give you,’ Eve said to Lyla as she went to unclasp the necklace from around her neck.

Lyla shook her head. ‘Keep it. It is yours and if we ever need you again make sure to wear it.’

‘It’s so beautiful, thank you,’ Eve breathed.

‘Thank you for everything, Eve.’ Lyla gave her friend a hug. ‘Now we no longer need to

live in fear of the pirates and the ocean can be at peace. No more unnatural tidal waves and gale force winds!'

'Where to now, Captain?' Oscar called from behind the wheel of the sloop.

Eve felt sad to leave but she had urgent unfinished business at home. 'Roche, the ship's all yours. Look after it.'

Roche saluted Eve and gave her a wink.

'I need to talk to Sylvie, Oscar. It's time to head home.'

***

Eve and Oscar gave their friends a final wave before they jumped off the ship and submerged into the deep water. Eve felt her body change, the colours looked less intense, the light less bright. When she realised she needed air she knew they were

home again. Eve pointed to the surface and she and Oscar emerged from the depths to see the coast of Marigold once again. They swam towards land and Eve was astonished to see that her clothes lay exactly where she had left them on the rocks.

The friends hurried home. Eve waved goodbye to Oscar and slipped into Sylvie's house through the back door. There was something she needed to check before she spoke to her grandmother.

Eve crept into Sylvie's room and opened her jewellery box. It was just as she'd remembered. Lying on top of a few chains was a mermaid necklace just like the one Eve had given Lyla. Eve knew for certain now that Sylvie had travelled to other worlds using the crystals.

'Gran?' she called. There was no answer. Eve searched each of the bedrooms, then

headed out to the front garden.

Sylvie was kneeling in front of her vegetable garden, pulling out weeds with a gardening fork.

'Gran!' Eve enveloped her grandmother in a hug from behind.

'Hello, dear,' said Sylvie, patting Eve's arm. 'I'm pleased you're here. I want to talk to you.' Sylvie took off her gardening gloves and sat beside Eve on the grass.

'I want to talk to you too,' said Eve. 'I'm sorry I hassled you.'

Sylvie held Eve's hand. 'No, Eve. You were right, I should have told you the truth. I just needed to be sure you were ready.'

'Ready for what?'

Sylvie's expression grew troubled. 'There is something very difficult and dangerous that needs to be done and I need your help.'

'Nothing can be worse than what I have

already faced.'

Sylvie shook her head. 'Do you remember me talking about the lacquered Chinese box in the attic?'

'Yes. You told me never to touch it.'

Sylvie squeezed Eve's hand. 'It is filled with the darkest magic imaginable. I can't put it off any longer. It's time to open the box and end this once and for all.'

Eve's eyes widened. Sylvie's hand shook in Eve's grasp.

What could possibly be in the box that made her gran so frightened?

About the Author

Jess Black enjoys writing stories with heaps of action and humour. She has previously co-written *The Bindi Wildlife Adventure Series*, a fictional series about helping endangered animals around the world.

Now available in the series

For more riddles and
adventures visit
www.keeperofthecrystals.com.au